ISBN: 9781955971003 (Paperback)
ISBN: 9781955971010 (Hardcover)
ISBN: 9781955971027 (Ebook)

Library of Congress Control Number: 2021916845

Disclaimer:
Portions of this book are works of fiction. Any references to historical events, real people, or real places are used fictitiously. Other names, characters, places and events are products of the author's imagination, and any resemblances to actual events or places or persons, living or dead, is entirely coincidental.

Acknowledgment:
Illustrator: Kai Hodge, Book Designer: Dasha Jensen, Editor: Rion Martin

Printed by IngramSpark, in the United States of America.

First printing, 2021.

www.tiffanytranbooks.com

Lily Lou AND THE GREAT APPLE SHORTAGE

by Tiffany Tran
Illustrated by Kai Hodge

Lily Lou and Jill were the best of friends.

Lily Lou loved to laugh.

Jill loved to smile.

But when Jill's grandpa passed away,
her smile also faded away.

Lily Lou wanted
to cheer Jill up.

So, she planned to
bake her a treat.

Jill's favorite dessert
was apple pie.

The next day,
Lily Lou woke up in shock.

She had planned to meet with Jill.

On the dot, at 3 o'clock.

Lily Lou sprinted
to the kitchen...

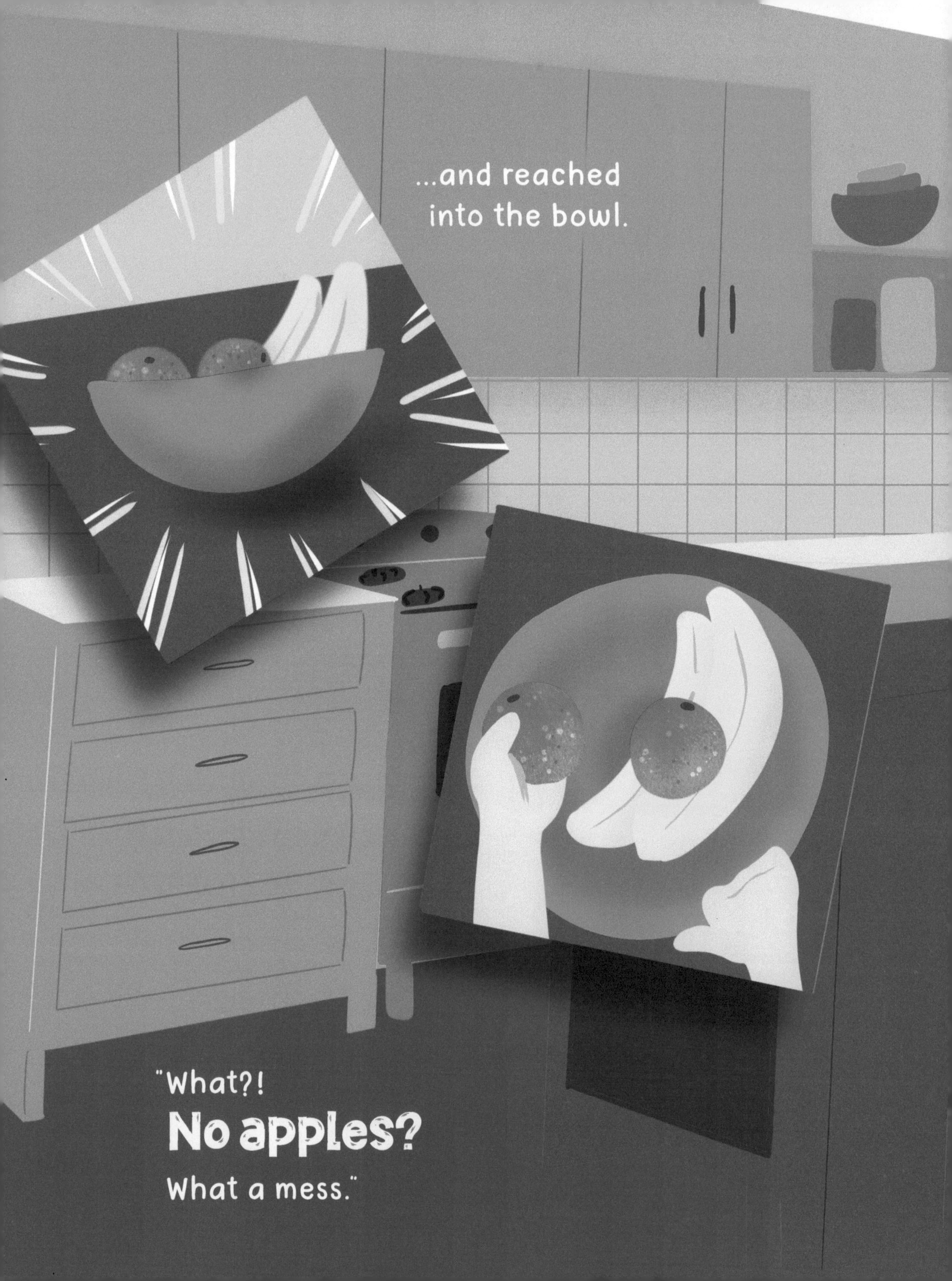

...and reached
into the bowl.

"What?!
No apples?
What a mess."

She slid across the kitchen floor and out
the door to find her neighbor, Mr. Jules.

"Good morning, Mr. Jules.
Do you have ten apples to spare?"
"Lily Lou, I have no apples to share.
Have you tried the Farmer's Market?
I bet you can find some there."

In a hurry, Lily Lou hopped on her bike.

She raced through
muddy puddles and kids
blowing bubbles.

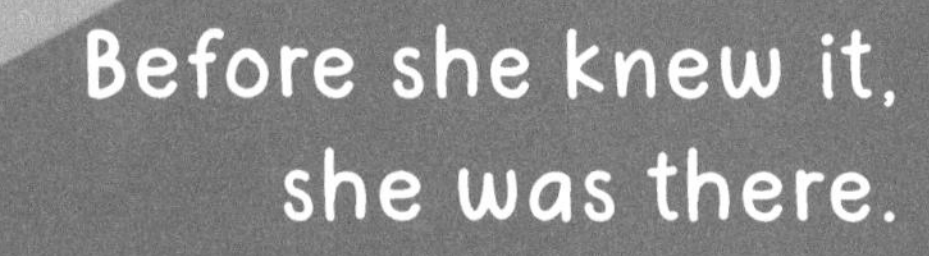

Before she knew it,
she was there.

In the distance, she saw a sign that read: "Bob's Apple Stand."

But as she got closer,
there was another
sign that said,
SOLD OUT!
Sold
Out
"Crunchy apple chips!
With no apples, how will
I bake this pie?"

Bob, the owner, kindly said, "Sorry kiddo.
For days, my apple supply has been dry.
The Big Market might be worth a try."

Fast as lightning, Lily Lou jumped back on her bike.

She dodged three jumpy cats and two stinky dumpsters.

Before she knew it, she had arrived.

Lily Lou saw:

Avocados, bananas, oranges, pears.

Pineapples, grapes, mangoes, coconuts.

Lemons, limes, strawberries, kiwi.

"...**But, no apples?**"

Not ready to give up without a fight, Lily Lou caught the store manager in her sight.

She ran over to her and said, "Do you have any apples in the back? I don't care if they're green or red."

The store manager replied, "The apple deliveries are late. I'm afraid you'll have to wait."

Lily Lou looked down at her watch and gasped,

"Crunchy apple chips!

So much time has passed.

I'm going to be late."

Swift like a donkey's kick, Lily Lou took off in a panic.

She steered past squirrelly squirrels and racing rabbits.

In a flash, she had arrived at Jill's grandpa's home at last.

And there at the window, Jill sat.

Quick like a cheetah, Jill ran to the door.

She had been patiently waiting all day to give Lily Lou a tour.

But before Jill could say anything, Lily Lou cried, "Jill. I'm so sorry. There were no apples to bake a pie. I tried. I asked Mr. Jules. I tried the Farmer's Market. I went to the Big Market. There were no more apples to buy."

Jill gave Lily Lou a comforting smile, then grabbed her by the hand, and said, "Follow me."

Confused, Lily Lou followed Jill into the house and back out the porch.

Standing side-by-side, they saw apple trees stretching far and wide.

Teary-eyed, Jill said, "Whenever grandpa finished his deliveries early, we would pick apples and make apple nachos together."

At that moment, Lily Lou realized
why apples were so hard to come by.
Jill's grandpa was the town's apple supply.
Without him, no apples could arrive.

They picked a few apples
together and ran back inside.

Jill looked at Lily Lou, held up two tasty apples, and said, "What are we going to do with these?"

Lily Lou's eyes lit up with excitement, like birthday candles, and said, "We are going to remember your grandpa."
She began searching the kitchen cabinets and pulled out...
a jar of peanut butter, chocolate chips, pretzels, and popcorn.
"Apple nachos!"
POP!
Pretzels!

Jill cracked a big smile.

This was the happiest Lily Lou had seen Jill in a while.

Jill set the apples down, gave Lily Lou a hug, and said, "I'm glad you're here with me right now.

An apple pie would have been nice but making apple nachos with you is an even better treat."

THE END

Movie Night Apple Nachos

Ingredients

- 2 granny smith apples
- 20 g of chocolate
- 2 tablespoons of peanut butter
- 1 handful of pretzels
- 1 handful of pop corn

Instructions

1. Cut the apples into slices and arrange them on a platter or plate.
2. Melt the chocolate in a double boiler or the microwave.
3. Microwave the peanut butter for a few seconds to make it runny and easy to drizzle.
4. Drizzle the chocolate and peanut butter onto the apple slices and add the pretzels and popcorn.
5. Enjoy!

serves 2

Sweet & Fruity Apple Nachos

Ingredients

- 2 gala apples
- 1 lemon
- 1 handful of raisins, cranberries or other dried fruit (goji berries, apricots, figs.)
- 2 tablespoons of unsweetened yogurt
- 1 handful of slivered almonds
- Maple syrup to taste

Instructions

1. Cut the apples into slices and arrange them on a platter or plate.
2. Mix the yogurt with the zest and juice of 1/2 a lemon.
3. Drizzle the lemony mixture onto the apple slices and add the raisins and almonds.
4. The gala apples are already quite sweet but feel free to add a drizzle of maple syrup for some extra sweetness.
5. Enjoy!

serves 2

Chocolate & Granola Apple Nachos

Ingredients

- 2 gala apples
- 20 g of chocolate
- Granola (store bought or homemade)

Instructions

1. Cut the apples into slices.
2. Melt the chocolate in a double boiler or the microwave. Dip the apple slices halfway into the chocolate and place them onto a baking sheet covered with parchment paper.
3. Add immediately the granola on top of the chocolate and let set in the fridge for 30 minutes.
4. Arrange the slices on a plate and enjoy!

serves 2

CPSIA information can be obtained
at www.ICGtesting.com
Printed in the USA
BVHW051601211221
624594BV00002B/62

* 9 7 8 1 9 5 5 9 7 1 0 0 3 *